To:

With love, from:

ALWAYS MORE LOVE

WORDS BY ERIN GUENDELSBERGER
PICTURES BY ANDOTWIN

sourcebooks
wonderland

I love you so much,
but there's more in my heart.
How is that possible?
Well, where do I start?

Now move in close, and you will see just how much you mean to me.

My love is huge—below, above.

As you can tell, there's always more love!

Is this the most that you can get?
Of course it's not. No way! Not yet!

Don't believe me? Let's try again.

Tickle here, beneath my chin.

Ha, ha, ha! It's no surprise—
with love there's joy, and it multiplies!
There always is more love, I say.
So please stop tickling now, okay?

I'm not just red—there's more to me.

Shake the book to see what I can be.

My love for you is rainbow bright—

it's green, blue, yellow, purple, white!

It's every shape and color too.

I always have more love for you!

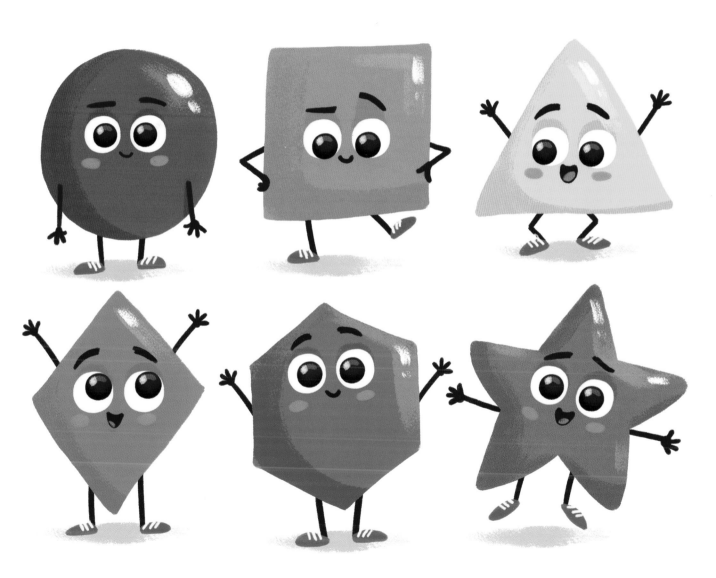

See the moon up in the sky?

Now trace its shape. I'll tell you why!

I love you to the moon and back—
from bluest sky to darkest black.

If we are near or far apart,
there's always more love in my heart.

Here's a door, but do you dare
to go *knock-knock* to see *who's there*?

It's me! I'm always here for you—
and full of love that's deep and true.
That's just another way to say
there's always more love every day.

Now make a face—as silly as you wish!

Now blow your biggest, loudest kiss!

Whoa! You knocked me off my feet
with kisses strong and oh-so-sweet.
I love you now—tomorrow too.
I'll always have more love for you!

You can grab the book and hug it tight
to squeeze out the love with all your might!
You can tip it over—point, push, and flip!
And still you'll always make my heart skip.

It doesn't matter what you do,
how much you ask—it's always true!
My love's an endless, open door.
I'll always love you more and more!

For Mike, my endless, open door.
—EG

For Rosco & Willow,
my paddy paw companions with the biggest hearts.
—AT

The art for this book was digitally sketched and colored using Wacom Cintiq and Adobe Photoshop.

Published by Sourcebooks Wonderland, an imprint of Sourcebooks Kids
P.O. Box 4410, Naperville, Illinois 60567-4410
(630) 961-3900
sourcebookskids.com

Library of Congress Cataloging-in-Publication Data is on file with the publisher.

Source of Production: Phoenix Color, Hagerstown, Maryland, USA
Date of Production: October 2021
Run Number: 5022995

Printed and bound in the United States of America.
PHC 10 9 8 7 6 5 4 3 2